ST. JOHN LUTHERAN SCHOOL
3521 Linda Vista Ave.
Napa, California 94558
(707) 226-7970

# LUCILLE

# LUCILLE

## STORY AND PICTURES BY

*Arnold Lobel*

AN I CAN READ BOOK

HARPER & ROW, PUBLISHERS
NEW YORK, EVANSTON, AND LONDON

# FOR SUSAN

This is Lucille.

Lucille belongs

to a farmer.

She pulls the farmer's plow

and works very hard

in the fields.

Sometimes Lucille sees herself
in a puddle.

It makes her sad.

"I am dull and dirty,"

says Lucille.

"What is wrong with being dirty?"
asks a small pig.
"I am dirty."

"Pigs are supposed to be
dirty," says Lucille.
"I'm tired of it."

This is the farmer's wife.

She sits in the house.

She drinks tea

and listens to the radio.

The farmer's wife likes Lucille.

"Lucille is a nice horse,"

says the farmer's wife

to the farmer.

"But she is dull and dirty."

21

One day the farmer's wife
comes to Lucille.
"Tomorrow we are going
shopping in town,"
she says.

Lucille takes the farmer
and his wife to town.

She sees a hat

with pink roses

in a store window.

The farmer's wife

buys the hat

for Lucille.

She sees many shiny shoes

in a store window.

The farmer's wife

buys four shiny shoes

for Lucille.

She sees a beautiful white dress

in a store window.

The farmer's wife

buys the dress

for Lucille.

"Look at Lucille,"

says the farmer's wife.

"Isn't she grand?"

"Yes," says the farmer sadly.

"She is too grand

to help me plow my fields."

The small pig

sees Lucille

coming down the road.

"What's all that stuff

you have on?" he says.

"These are my new clothes
and now I'm a lady,
so get out of my way,"
snorts Lucille.

Now Lucille does not work

in the fields.

She sits in the house

in her hat, in her shoes,

and in her dress.

She drinks tea

and listens to the radio

with the farmer's wife.

The pink roses on Lucille's hat
tickle her,
the shiny shoes hurt her feet,
and her beautiful white dress
makes her hot.
Lucille wishes she were outside
working with the farmer.

"Today we are having a party,"

says the farmer's wife.

"All the ladies

want to meet you, Lucille."

Soon some ladies

come to meet Lucille.

More and more ladies
come to meet Lucille.
"Isn't she lovely,"
they say.

One lady brings Lucille flowers.

"Thank you," says Lucille,

and she eats them.

"Lucille!" calls the farmer's wife.

"Ladies do not eat flowers.

They smell them."

Soon the room

is crowded.

All the ladies are drinking tea

and eating cookies.

They are talking very loudly.

They make Lucille nervous.

Lucille steps

on her beautiful white dress

and tears it.

She bumps into a lady

and knocks her down.

"Excuse me," says Lucille,

but she knocks down

two more ladies.

Lucille's hat

falls over her eyes.

She breaks the teapot

and spills the cookies.

"Help, help!" cry the ladies.

"Lucille, you are not

being ladylike!"

shouts the farmer's wife.

"I am not a lady,"
cries Lucille.
"I am a horse!"

She knocks down

five more ladies

and runs out of the house.

Lucille runs and runs.

She runs into the fields.

She kisses the farmer because
she is glad to see him again.

She kisses the pig

because he is dirty.

That night Lucille

eats the pink roses

and the hat for supper.

"I am glad

to be a plain, happy horse,"

she says.

And then she goes to sleep.